KU-712-196

Contents

by Maureen Spurgeon

© 1994 Brown Watson, England

TELL ME A STORY

Brown Watson

ENGLAND

Pinocchio

Geppetto was a poor toymaker whose dearest wish was to have a son. One day, as he sat making a wooden puppet, it seemed to look at him and to smile. "How I wish I could look on the face of my son," he said. "I would call him Pinocchio."

Geppetto did not know it, but the
Blue Fairy had heard what he said.
"He deserves to have his wish
granted," she thought. "Pinocchio
shall be a son to Geppetto."

And, as Pinocchio's eyes opened wide, so there came a chirruping noise from the fireplace. "Meet Jiminy Cricket!" said the fairy. "He is your conscience to tell you right from wrong, Pinocchio."

Geppetto was overjoyed to have a son at last! "You must go to school, Pinocchio," he said.

"That's right!" nodded Jiminy Cricket. "Otherwise, you'll turn into a donkey."

Geppetto even sold his only jacket so that he could afford to buy Pinocchio the spelling book he needed to take to school.

"Goodbye, Father!" he called. "I shall make you proud of me."

But that was before Pinocchio knew Fire-Eater's Puppet Theatre was in town! Taking no notice of Jiminy Cricket, he sold his book to buy a ticket – and soon he was on stage, singing and dancing.

Fire-Eater wanted Pinocchio to stay. But when the time came to move far away from home and Geppetto, he was afraid. Being a wonderful singing, dancing puppet didn't seem so clever, after all. . .

"Geppetto sold his jacket to send me to school," he sobbed to Jiminy Cricket. "He'll wonder where I am!"

Luckily for him, Fire-Eater knew Geppetto and he gave Pinocchio five pieces of gold to take home.

"I can buy Geppetto a new jacket," cried Pinocchio. "Five gold pieces!"

"Is that all?" scoffed a cat.

"Bury them in our magic field," said the fox with him. "You'll have a tree of gold next day!"

"No, Pinocchio!" said Jiminy Cricket. "That's Geppetto's money!"

How Pinocchio wished he had listened to Jiminy when he discovered that the crafty cat and the sly fox had dug up the gold he had buried!

The fairy heard Pinocchio crying and asked him what was wrong.

"I dropped the gold I was taking home to Geppetto," he sobbed. "Now I can't find it!" And as he spoke, something very strange happened. . .

Pinocchio's nose began to grow!
"Where do you think you lost the money?" asked the fairy.
"On the way to school," he cried.
His nose grew even longer!
"It fell out of my pocket."

By now, his nose was so long, he could hardly see the end of it!

"Well, Pinocchio," laughed the Blue Fairy, "now you know how one small lie can grow into a big lie – just like your nose!"

At once, Pinocchio promised not to tell any more lies, sobbing so hard that the fairy took pity on him. "If you had listened to Jiminy Cricket," she said, "none of this would have happened !"

Pinocchio knew this was true, and, full of good intentions, he set off home. He had only gone a little way when a carriage full of children came along, pulled by some strange-looking donkeys!

"Come to the Land of Toys and play all the year round!" they cried. "Don't listen to them," warned Jiminy Cricket. But Pinocchio was already jumping up, determined not to miss any of the fun.

He thought the Land of Toys was wonderful! No books, no lessons – just as much play as anyone wanted!

But after a while, he noticed his ears felt rather heavy – heavy and long, thick and furry . . .

"I said that you'd turn into a donkey if you didn't go to school," scolded Jiminy Cricket. "What will you do, now?"

"Geppetto!" cried Pinocchio. "I want to go home to Geppetto!"

Pinocchio was afraid everyone would laugh at his donkey ears. But the people were too upset even to notice. "Geppetto went to sea, looking for you," they said. "We think he was swallowed by a whale!"

"Poor Father," cried Pinocchio. "I must find him!" He made his way to the place where Geppetto was last seen and jumped into the inky blackness of the sea, gusts of wind hitting him in the face.

Suddenly, he saw a light ahead. He swam towards it and found himself crawling, then walking into a sort of underground cavern. "Pinocchio!" cried a voice. "Pinocchio, my dear, brave son!"

Pinocchio had never been so glad to see anyone – even if he had swum inside a whale by mistake!

"We'll get through the whale's mouth, then make for the shore," he told Geppetto. "Just follow me!"

When the whale opened its mouth, they quickly swam out! But Pinocchio was soon very tired, swimming for Geppetto as well as himself. By the time Jiminy Cricket had guided him to dry land, he could hardly move.

The Blue Fairy was waiting when Geppetto carried him to dry land.

"Well done, Pinocchio," she said. "You have shown that you are a brave and loving son. You shall have your reward!"

And instead of a little wooden puppet, Pinocchio became a real boy with a beaming smile for Geppetto – and a conscience of his own to tell him right from wrong. How happy Jiminy Cricket was for both his friends!

Alice in Wonderland

Alice was tired of sitting on the bank. The sun made her feel sleepy. Suddenly a white rabbit ran past saying, "Oh, dear! Oh, dear! I shall be too late!" and taking a watch from his waistcoat pocket!

Alice had never seen a white rabbit with a waistcoat, or a pocket watch, so she followed him to see where he was going. And when the White Rabbit went down a rabbit hole – down went Alice after it.

Suddenly, Alice felt herself falling, down, down, down . . . until, thump! She landed on a heap of dry leaves. "Oh, my ears and whiskers!" she heard the White Rabbit saying. "How late it is getting!"

All at once, he vanished from sight – leaving Alice in a long, low hall with locked doors all around. Alice came across a little table on which there was a key. But, which door did it fit?

Then she came across a tiny door behind a curtain. She turned the key in the lock, and the door opened. Kneeling down, she could see a beautiful garden, with bright flower beds and water fountains.

"Now," thought Alice, "how do I get out?" On the table where the key had been there was a bottle with "DRINK ME!" written on a label around the neck – it was the most delicious drink Alice had ever tasted!

And with every drop, Alice became smaller and smaller – until she was just the right size to get through the little door and into the beautiful garden. If only she had not left the key on the table . . .

Then, she found a box with a cake inside. In currants were the words, "EAT ME." So, Alice did, growing taller and taller – until she was much too big to go through the door, even though she had the key!

Alice was so sad, she began to cry. Before long, there was the patter of feet and in came the White Rabbit. The sight of such a big, tall Alice frightened him so much, he dropped the fan and gloves he was carrying.

Alice picked up the fan, quickly dropping it when she found herself shrinking again! Her foot slipped, and – splash! She was up to her chin in the pool of tears she had wept when she had been so tall.

In the pool of tears were also a duck, a dodo – and a mouse who told a story to get everyone dry!

"Mary Ann!" called a voice. "Fetch me my gloves this minute!" It was the White Rabbit.

This time, Alice followed him to a little house with "W. RABBIT" on the door. Coming out the other side, she saw a huge mushroom, about as tall as she was now, on which a caterpillar sat, smoking a pipe!

The caterpillar said that eating one side of the mushroom would make her taller, the other side smaller. So Alice took a piece of each. A Cheshire Cat grinned at her from a tree.

"Please," said Alice to the cat, "which way should I go?"

"That way," said the cat waving his right paw, "lives the Mad Hatter, and that way," waving his other paw, "lives the March Hare!"

The March Hare's house had a roof thatched with fur and chimneys shaped like long ears! He and the Mad Hatter sat outside at a table, resting their elbows on a very sleepy dormouse.

"Tell us a story!" ordered the March Hare.

"Well," said Alice, taken by surprise, "I don't think . . ."

"Don't think?" he echoed. "Then you shouldn't talk!"

That was enough to make Alice march away from the table. Quite by chance she saw one of the trees had a door set in it. When Alice opened it, she was in the hall again.

Nibbling one piece of the caterpillar's mushroom, then the other, Alice made herself the right size to get the key, then go through the little door and out into the beautiful garden, at last!

In the garden, two gardeners were painting white roses red! "We planted a white rose by mistake!" explained one, "and if the queen finds out . . . . Oh no! Here she comes  now!"

The Queen of Hearts stopped when she saw Alice. "What is your name, child?" she asked.

"My name," said Alice, "is Alice."

"Can you play croquet?"

"Oh, yes!" cried Alice.

52

Alice had never played croquet using flamingoes to hit curled-up hedgehogs! Before long the game was a real mess, with the queen yelling "Off with his head!" or "Off with her head!" every other minute.

Suddenly, Alice heard a cry.
"The trial is beginning!"
"What trial?" asked Alice – but everyone was already running ahead, carrying her along with them into a big court room.

"The charge is," said the White
Rabbit, "that the Knave of Hearts
stole some tarts!"

"Call the first witness!" said the
king. And to her great surprise, the
White Rabbit called, "Alice!"

"What do you know of this?" asked the king.

"Nothing whatsoever," said Alice.

"Off with her head!" shouted the Queen of Hearts, red in the face.

"You?" went on Alice. "You're only a pack of cards!"

At once, the cards rose up and came flying down on her! Alice gave a little scream – and found herself on the bank with her sister.

Her adventures in Wonderland had only been a wonderful dream!

The Ugly Duckling

Mother Duck had found the perfect place on the farm to build her nest. It was next to a little stream. The other ducks quacked and splashed about in the water, as she sat waiting for her eggs to hatch.

Then, at last, came the great day when the shells burst open, one after the other!

"Cheep-Cheep!" piped the tiny, yellow ducklings as they waddled around. "How wide the world is!"

Mother Duck fussed round them proudly. She was so busy trying to keep all her ducklings together, that, at first, she did not notice there was one egg, bigger than any of the others, still in the nest.

"That's a turkey's egg!" quacked
an old duck when she saw it. "And
turkeys never learn to swim, my
dear, not like our little ones. Nasty
birds, they are, too! Take my advice
and leave it alone."

But Mother Duck said she would sit on the egg a little longer until it hatched. And, instead of a pretty, yellow duckling, out came a fat, ugly chick with horrible dark grey feathers!

"Was this really a turkey chick?" wondered Mother Duck, leading the way down to the stream. How glad she was to see the ugly, little bird swimming along behind the others.

"He's not a turkey," she thought, "just an Ugly Duckling."

The Ugly Duckling soon began to grow, and as he grew, the uglier he became. The other ducklings wouldn't even talk to him.

The hens in the farmyard pecked at him whenever he came near. Worst of all was the turkey cock, who came at the Ugly Duckling making loud gobbling noises, until it was red in the face.

Even the little girl who fed the farmyard birds aimed kicks at him. Unhappy and frightened, he flew off, some smaller birds getting out of his way. "That's because I'm so ugly," he thought.

The Ugly Duckling flew on until he came to a marsh where some wild ducks lived.

"My," said one, "you're so ugly!"

The Ugly Duckling just fluffed up his feathers and fell asleep.

Next day, the air was shattered by hunters shooting at the wild ducks. The Ugly Duckling thought he would die when one of the dogs found him. Then – splash – the dog turned and went.

"I'm so ugly!" thought the Ugly Duckling. "Even the dog does not bite me." And he went on his way, until he came to a hut where an old woman lived with her cat and a hen. He crept inside.

The woman thought the Ugly Duckling was a lady duck to lay eggs for her. But as he grew fatter and uglier and no eggs came, she got angry. The hen and cat hated him because he could swim.

All through the summer the Ugly Duckling was all alone, eating whatever he could find. Then came the autumn, when the leaves blew down from the trees and the clouds hung low in the sky.

Then, at sunset one day, the Ugly Duckling saw the most beautiful white birds flying across the lake. He watched them until they were out of sight, wishing with all his heart that he could be with them.

The winter snow reminded him of those beautiful white birds. The river froze, almost freezing the Ugly Duckling with it, until a kind man broke the ice and took him home.

His children wanted to play, but the Ugly Duckling thought they would hurt him. They scared him so much that he splashed into a pail of milk, and then into a barrel of oatmeal!

The man's children laughed and laughed, but their mother was furious. The Ugly Duckling only just missed being hit by the fire tongs, as he ran out into the bitter winter weather.

Now came the worst part of the Ugly Duckling's whole life. Often he felt he would die from hunger and cold, longing for some shelter. He could hardly believe it when the sun shone again and the birds sang.

Hearing the birds, the Ugly Duckling flapped his own wings, surprised to find how big and strong they had become. The sun warmed his back as he flew, making him feel

happier than he had been for a long, long time.

On and on flew the Ugly Duckling until he saw a garden, the scent of flowers wafting up towards him. Suddenly, three beautiful white swans flew out from the thicket, gliding into the water.

These were the birds he had seen in the autumn, the ones he loved – although he did not know why. "What if they hurt me?" he thought. "Better to die here than to be beaten and punished because I'm so ugly . . ."

Slowly, the swans turned and came towards him, looking so solemn that the Ugly Duckling bowed his head. He saw his reflection in the water – not the reflection of an Ugly Duckling but of a beautiful white swan.

The Ugly Duckling thought he was dreaming! Could he really be a beautiful swan?

"There's a new swan! Isn't he lovely?" said some children as they stood by   the lake

The handsome young swan lifted his head, looking all around him.

"This cannot be a dream," he thought. "I could never, ever have dreamed of being so happy when I was the Ugly Duckling!"

Goldilocks

and the Three Bears

There was once a girl whose hair was so fair and curly, that everyone called her Goldilocks.

Goldilocks and her family lived near a forest, and she liked nothing better than going for long walks on her own.

Goldilocks thought she must
know every inch of that forest until,
one morning, after she had set off
a little earlier than usual, she saw
something which gave her quite a
surprise. . .

It was a little cottage she had never seen before, with lace curtains at the windows and smoke coming out of the chimney.

"Who can live here?" wondered Goldilocks, going up to the door.

She knocked at the door and waited. There was no answer. She knocked again. Still, no answer.

"Anyone at home?" she called, and knocked again, a little harder this time. The door creaked open.

Goldilocks stepped inside and looked all round such a cosy, little room. A fire burned cheerfully, and on the hob were three bowls of porridge – a big bowl, a smaller bowl, and a tiny, little bowl. . .

"I wonder who lives here?" thought Goldilocks again, never guessing it was the home of three bears – Daddy Bear, Mummy Bear and Baby Bear. She only knew how good that porridge looked on a fresh, spring morning.

First she tasted Daddy Bear's porridge. That was too hot. Then, she tried Mummy Bear's porridge. That was too cold. But when she tasted Baby Bear's porridge, it was so good that Goldilocks soon ate it all up!

After eating all that porridge, Goldilocks wanted to sit down. So she tried Daddy Bear's chair. That was too hard. Then she tried Mummy Bear's chair, but that was too soft. Then, she tried Baby Bear's chair. . .

And that was just right! In fact, Goldilocks had never sat in such a comfortable chair! She wriggled and squirmed so much, that, in the end, the chair broke, and Goldilocks fell to the floor!

"Ooh!" she groaned. "I think I'd better go and lie down." So, she went upstairs.

And in the bedroom were three beds — Daddy Bear's bed, Mummy Bear's bed, and Baby Bear's bed. . .

First, she tried Daddy Bear's bed.
But that was too hard. Then she tried
Mummy Bear's bed. That was too soft.
But Baby Bear's bed was so warm and
so cosy that Goldilocks snuggled
down and was soon fast asleep!

By this time, Daddy Bear, Mummy
Bear and Baby Bear were coming
back from their walk. They had only
gone to the end of the forest path
and back – "Just to let the porridge
cool down," Mummy Bear had said.

"Who's been eating my porridge?" growled Daddy Bear.

"Who's been eating my porridge?" said Mummy Bear.

"Who's been eating my porridge?" cried Baby Bear. "There's none left!"

"And who's been sitting in my chair?" roared Daddy Bear.

"Who's been sitting in my chair?" cried Mummy Bear.

"Who's been sitting in my chair?" wailed Baby Bear. "It's all broken!"

They went upstairs. "Who's been sleeping in my bed?" said Daddy Bear.

"Who's been sleeping in my bed?" squealed Mummy Bear.

"Who's been sleeping in my bed?" said Baby Bear, with a loud sob.

His cries woke Goldilocks and she sat straight up in bed. She could not believe her eyes when she saw three furry faces looking at her! "B-bears!" she blurted out, very frightened. "Th-three b-bears!"

Had Goldilocks known it, Daddy, Mummy and Baby Bear were gentle, kind bears. When they saw it was only a little girl who had been in their cottage, they were not nearly so angry as they might have been.

But Goldilocks only knew that she had to leave their cottage just as soon as she could. So she let out a scream, the loudest, longest scream she had ever screamed, making the Three Bears jump back at once!

This was Goldilocks' chance! She flung back the bedclothes and rushed out of the door and down the stairs, away back into the forest before the Three Bears knew what was happening!

On and on she ran through the forest until she felt she could run no more. It seemed a long, long time before she reached the path which led to her own home.

And there was her mother, waiting

anxiously at the gate. Goldilocks was so glad to see her.

"Oh, where have you been, Goldilocks?" she cried. "Daddy was just going out to look in the forest for you!"

And so began the story of Goldilocks and the Three Bears. Her mother could hardly believe it!

"You naughty girl!" she scolded. "Haven't I always told you never to go inside strange places?"

"Goldilocks," said her daddy, "are you sure this tale about The Three Bears isn't an excuse because you do not know the forest as well as you thought?"

"No, Daddy," cried Goldilocks.

"Here," she went on, taking his hand, "I'll take you to their cottage, myself. Then you'll see."

And she quickly led the way back into the forest without stopping once, seeming sure of every step.

That was the first of many times Goldilocks went back to the forest. But, no matter how hard she searched, she did not find that little cottage, nor The Three Bears – Daddy Bear, Mummy Bear and Baby Bear.